This igloo book belongs to:

Charlotte Lister

igloobooks

Published in 2014
by Igloo Books Ltd
Cottage Farm
Sywell
NN6 0BJ
www.igloobooks.com

Copyright © 2014 Igloo Books Ltd

FIR003 0114
2 4 6 8 10 9 7 5 3 1
ISBN 978-1-78197-625-8

Illustrated by Tom Knight

Printed and manufactured in China

The Naughtiest Fairy

Tom Knight

igloobooks

In Miss Magic's fairy class, most of the fairies were as sweet as sugarplums, but one was not quite as sweet as she appeared to be.

Her name was **Fairy Trixi.**

Trixi was the **naughtiest** fairy in the whole of Fairyland and she loved to play jokes on all her friends.

With every **Swish** of Trixi's magical wand, mischief was sure to follow.

The other fairies loved their
magic lessons in fairy school,
but Trixi found them
boring.

She would **secretly** cast a spell on the classroom clock to make the hands move faster.

TICK! TOCK!

Tick! Tock!

Tick! Tock!

TICK! TOCK!

Poor Miss Magic would think it was already lunchtime and would shoo all the little fairies off to eat.

One morning, when Trixi was feeling even more bored than usual, Miss Magic asked the fairies to turn to the page about frogs in their spell books.

This gave Trixi a rather **naughty** idea.

She swooshed her wand.

ZIIING!

Suddenly, frogs leapt out of the pages and across the classroom. "Oh, my goodness!" cried Miss Magic, in fright.

Later that morning, Trixi had another naughty idea. "I'm going to turn everyone's fairy dust into sneezing powder," she said,

waving her wand.

Achoo!

Trixi laughed, gleefully, as all the little fairies rolled about, sneezing uncontrollably.

Trixi fluttered off happily to see what other mischief she could get up to.

"Something **really** needs to be done about Trixi," said Bella, rubbing her itchy nose and sniffing.

"Don't worry," replied Lily, noticing that Trixi had left her magic wand on a toadstool nearby. "I have an idea!"

HonK!

She **waved** her own wand and began to cast a special spell.

After lunch, Trixi returned to the classroom. "I'm going to make it rain inside," she thought.

She **aimed** her wand at the ceiling.

To her astonishment,
hundreds
of
sweets
began
to
land
everywhere!

"**Hooray!**"
the fairies
shouted.

Trixi frowned. "Alright," she thought. "This time, I'm going to make everyone's chairs disappear. That will be really funny!" She chuckled to herself as she **waved** her wand once more.

ZIIING!

Every chair in the classroom turned into a **lovely,**

comfy,

beanbag.
Trixi's friends were very pleased.

The last lesson of the day was the flying lesson. "I'm going to shrink everyone's wings so they all fall over," said Trixi. She gave her wand the biggest

swoosh

she could give.

With a **flash,** all the fairies' wings grew really big and beautiful.

"Oh, thank you, Trixi!"

they all shouted excitedly, as they soared high in the sky on their fabulous wings.

Trixi was **very** confused.

The fairies finished flying and landed gently next to Trixi,
who was looking quite sad. "What's wrong?" asked Lily.
"We think your spells have been

wonderful!"

"None of my spells are working properly," moaned Trixi. "I don't know what's going on."

When Trixi's friends saw she had learned her lesson, they felt a little bit sorry for her, so Lily explained what had happened.

"I'm sorry we played a trick on you," she said, smiling, "but we all **love** your kind and helpful spells!"

"Yes, I guess they were more fun than my naughty spells," agreed Trixi, with a grin.

With a swish, Lily removed the spell from Trixi's wand.
"I think I've learned my lesson," laughed Trixi.
"I promise I won't play tricks on anyone ever again."